Advance praise for
Just a Penny's Worth

"*Just a Penny's Worth* is a delightful collection of people, places and reflections. It appeals to young and old alike. It is full of wonderful characters, easily imagined through the author's descriptions. Reading about someone else's memories can trigger your own. Everyone can relate to remembering one's own childhood."

Terresa Cook, English teacher/parent, Vacaville, CA

"Penny's stories are woven with engaging warmth that will stir up memories from your own childhood. She produces the fun and joy that children have, as well as the vivid characteristics about family and neighbors that have left lasting impressions on us all."

Judi Anderson, Director of Continuing Education
Paradise Valley Community College, Arizona

Illustrated.
by our friend
Shirley Fulcher (N.E.)
2005

Just a Penny's Worth

Growing up in New York in the 1940s

by Penny Albright Petersen

Illustrations by Shirley Fulcher

Just a Penny's Worth
ISBN #0-9655696-1-5

Published by Desert State Publishing
9834 East Watford Way
Sun Lakes, AZ 85248

Printed in USA through the publisher's agency,
OPA Publishing
A division of Optimum Performance Associates
Box 12354
Chandler, AZ 85248-0023
E-mail: info@opapublishing.com
Online at: http://www.opapublishing.com

Table of Contents

Dedication

This book is dedicated to

Shelby Anne Steiner
and
Nicholas Scott Steiner
for whom I began writing these stories

and

for the enjoyment of my other grandchildren
Reed Hutchinson Steiner
Bennett John Steiner
Samuel Barton Steiner
Ashley Marie Petersen

Introduction

Once, a long time ago, (October 27, 1937, to be exact) a tiny, baby girl was born in New Jersey. She was supposed to arrive in January, but she was in a hurry. She was very, very little, just over three pounds. She had to stay in the hospital a long time. The nurses told the baby's mother, "You didn't get a whole baby, you got 'just a penny's worth.'" So they called her 'Penny,' even though her legal name was Janet Lois, after her aunt.

These stories represent the remembrances of Penny Albright from the earliest time she could recall until age 11. They take place in and around the city of New York and are told from the child's point of view. Childhood memories being what they are, sometimes chunks of time evaporate or obvious details cannot be recalled, so the stories may be slightly embellished. Please enjoy.

Penny Janet Lois Albright Steiner Petersen

Moving

New York City

Moving

Almost every year, sometimes twice a year, our family moved. But we always stayed close to New York City, where my father worked. The first house I remember had a huge porch with lots of windows. Because I had asthma, I couldn't go outside except in good weather. The porch made it like being outside. Mom and I built things with blocks, drew pictures, and played games on the porch. A few times other kids came over, but the girls always wanted to play dolls. I hated dolls. I liked Tinker Toys, zoo animals, modeling clay and dress-up.

Mom said the heating bills were too expensive because of all the windows, so we moved to Grandma Hutchinson's house in Caldwell, New Jersey, for a while. I liked it there. Grandma took me grocery shopping and let me pick out the dessert. Grandpa took me for long walks in the park where flowers and grass grew everywhere. I learned to ride a bike.

We were there half the winter and one summer. Then we moved to an apartment in New York City. No grass there. There were lots of other apartments all around us and they all looked the same. It would have been easy to get lost, so I stayed close to Mom. My dad decided we needed a yard and some space, so off we went to Mt. Kisco in the country. Our house was at the top of a wonderful hill, but it was too far for dad to go to work. Finally, we moved to Carl Place, Long Island, and dad rode the train into the city every day.

I can't remember every place we lived. Mostly, I remember moving vans and a heavy piano. Every time we moved, Mom got out all the blankets in the house and put them over and around that piano. Then she kept her hands steering it as the men took it down the walk and lifted it into the huge truck. Then she stuffed towels and sheets between the piano and whatever was next to it. Then she worried. She worried about that piano every minute until the truck arrived at the new place.

When the truck door lifted, she watched as beds and chairs and china and lamps came out. But she didn't much care about those. She didn't care much about my toys either. But, as soon as she saw that piano, she got excited. She'd put her hand on it over all the blankets and walk with it into the new house.

As soon as the workers got it in place, she examined every key, especially the black ones. Those were her favorites. She said the black ones made sounds that got into your heart. After she'd checked over the keys, she'd sit down and play things. If the moving went OK, she played pretty classical music with fingers dashing over the notes. If she ended up mad, she'd pound the keys hard and hold her foot down on the pedal.

The time we moved into the apartment, we had to leave the piano at Grandma's house. Mother was not happy. I was happy. When you looked out the window, you could see tall buildings and lots of stores with people walking in and out. At night, there were millions of lights everywhere. It felt like being up with the stars.

I also liked the elevator. Two rows of buttons begged for me to press them. When I did, the light would go on and the elevator would go up or down. At first, I couldn't count very well, so I didn't know which was higher 12 or 21. After a while, I got the hang of it. I learned to count to 29 way before the kids who lived in New Jersey.

The apartment was close to dad's job, but Mom was not happy. She wanted to live where she could take my baby brother, Lew, outside to play. We moved again. But that time the piano came, too. In fact, from then on the piano always came—until we moved out West.

 "Little" Grandma

Little Grandma

My "Little Grandma," Gertrude Hutchinson, was four foot, ten and a half inches tall, almost. "Big Grandma" was six feet tall. My brother, Lew, and I always called them "Big" and "Little" Grandma. Even Mom and Dad did it. But Grandma Hutchinson hated it. She would never allow her picture to be taken with "Big Grandma."

We tried hard not to call her "Little Grandma" when she was around, but sometimes we'd forget. Then we'd get a big, long lecture about proper behavior for polite children.

"Little Grandma" lived in New Jersey most of the time. She also had a summerhouse in Silver Beach, New York. When we were there, "Little Grandma" was fun. She loved sitting on the deck overlooking the river and talking to the neighbors. She made peanut butter cookies and lemonade. If Lew and I made friends with other kids, she'd say, "Invite them over for a cookie."

But at the big house in Caldwell, New Jersey, everything was strict. There were pretty glass candles and nut dishes on the coffee table. The adults drank coffee from cups with hand painted flowers and gold trim around the edges. Each person had a cup with a different flower so nobody gave germs to anyone else. Grandma's eyes got big and buggy when my brother walked near the coffee table. She'd rush over and put away her favorite glass candlesticks then huff away muttering.

Shopping was Grandma's hobby. She didn't like baseball or track, but she could walk five or six miles through Macy's or Bloomingdale's and never get tired. She flitted from counter to counter with mom, Lew and me trailing behind her like a slow dragon's tail. She picked up this and that -- a red scarf, but it was too little; a pair of tan gloves, but they were too big; a nightdress, a gold hair clip with fake diamonds, a notepad that said "Dear Friends," in flowery script. Each was turned over, examined, hummed over, her face squinched up with thoughtfulness. Each was returned to its place with a small upward twitch of the head, meaning it wouldn't do.

Then she'd get to me. I loved the walking. Even examining each item wasn't bad, although I wasn't allowed to touch anything even though she touched everything at least three times. But when she wanted to buy me something, it was always the same. She'd pick out the most frilly, lacy dress she could find. And she always found it on the rack with the smallest size.

Then she'd say, "Oh, Penny, this is so adorable, it looks just like you."

She was wrong.

I was chubby, had pigtails and was a tomboy. She wanted me to be Shirley Temple. Each time, when I was about dissolved into tears, she'd say, "Well, all right! You pick out something yourself. We'll compromise." Compromise meant I couldn't get pants, which was what I wanted, and she couldn't get me a frilly dress, which was what she wanted me to have.

When shopping ceased, we'd go for dessert.

"I'm dieting, but for this special occasion, I'm having something good," she'd exclaim. Lew always got chocolate ice cream. Grandma got some kind of pie with ice cream and chocolate sauce on top. Mom got coffee. I mostly had coconut cream pie. We laughed and ate. Dessert made shopping and the frilly dresses just a minor part of "Little Grandma."

"B I G" Grandma

Big Grandma

"Big Grandma," Viola Albright, stretched six feet tall. She was only one inch shorter than my dad. She and grandpa Charlie would sometimes keep me for the weekend. Whenever that happened, I'd get to push the elevator button to #5 and ring the apartment bell. I'd hear her coming—clack, clack, clack—over the wooden floor. She'd look through that funny peek-hole in the door that made her eye look bigger than it really was. When she opened the door the light framed her. Even though I'd seen her open the door many times, it always startled me. If it weren't for the big smile, the sight of her six-foot frame would have sent me running.

"Big Grandma" always wore an apron and funny 'clack-clack' shoes. They tied like tennis shoes, but they were white leather and had high heels. The clack-clack shoes made her look even bigger. They were oh-so-much bigger than any shoes I'd ever seen! Size 11. But one didn't ask about her big shoes or about why we had to do dishes before playing cards. One just obeyed. That's the way it was.

"Big Grandma's" apartment was like a museum. There were delicate china dishes trimmed in gold leaves, a Dutch cabinet she painted herself with bright blue birds each holding flowers in their mouths, a blue and yellow vase with carved children at the base. Tiny little spoons with pictures on them hung in neat rows all across the yellow kitchen. A china oriental cat sat on the second shelf of an antique bookshelf along with crystal goblets and cut glass birds. I so wanted to play with that cat. I always stood several minutes staring at it, but I was never allowed.

I did get to set the table with the white lace tablecloth Grandma crocheted herself. It had ever so many snowflakes all sewed together. When we had dinner, she put it over a dark blue tablecloth. Then all the delicate china and tiny silver spoons and glasses that sounded like birds singing all sat on the table.

"Big Grandma's" apartment was in Parkchester, New York. It smelled sweet, like chocolate or tapioca pudding. The yellow teapot always steamed hot water, and the oven baked unbelievable chocolate coconut cookies. Melting sweetly in my mouth, those cookies filled me with toasty contentment.

A constant stream of Grandma's friends came calling. She'd let them in, with her apron on and her clack, clack shoes. Then we'd sip tea and eat two cookies, never three or four. The ladies would talk a while, hug, and be gone. In the afternoon, we'd sit at the card table and play Yahtzee or Canasta. She tried very hard to teach me how to shuffle cards with a whirring sound, but I couldn't manage it.

"Big Grandma" liked to sing. She sang the Lord's Prayer every Sunday at the huge Lutheran Church down the street. When we sang together we sang "Row, Row Your Boat," "Silent Night" and "Jesus Loves Me." When I was 10, she taught me "Oh, Holy Night." There were lots of high notes. I couldn't get to those, but she'd open her mouth, looking like an angel, and the apartment filled with sound. When she sang, she wasn't "Big Grandma," she was bright light and shining eyes and music floating through my heart.

Birthday Brat

Birthday Brat

"Little Grandma" was excited about having my fifth birthday party at her house in New Jersey. The trees glowed in fall orange and yellow. There were red paper flowers on the front door. Red was my favorite color. "Little Grandma" had red decorations on the kitchen table, two kinds of lemonade, a big chocolate cake decorated with red flowers, and three kinds of ice cream in the refrigerator. She liked chocolate. Gramps liked strawberry. My mother and brother liked vanilla.

The dining room table looked like it grew presents—big ones with bows, little ones with ribbons, and a strange, flat one that was square and fascinating. The square package turned into a problem.

I wanted that package right now! I knew that opening packages waited until after everybody ate cake and sang "Happy Birthday." But I didn't want to open all the packages; I just wanted the square one. So I went to the dining room table and announced to my parents, grandparents and little friends that I was going to open this <u>one</u> package right now.

I got pretty much what I wanted, so I was surprised when my Grandfather, who was usually very quiet, said, "No presents until after the cake." If my father had said it in his strong, deep tone, as he did when he'd say, "Are you going to behave or do you want the hairbrush?" I probably would have stopped. But I just couldn't believe my quiet, sweet Gramps wouldn't let me have what I wanted. So I walked over and picked up the package. As I started to rip off the huge, red ribbon covering almost the whole top of the square, my Grandfather picked me up, took the package out of my hand, and set me down bluntly.

I screamed and cried as if the big, bad wolf had just come through the door. Everyone tried to shut me up. My grandmother pleaded. My father glared. My grandfather got redder and redder in the face. My mother squatted down and said commandingly, "If you don't stop this tantrum, we're going to take you home right now, and your friends can enjoy your birthday party without you!"

I whined, "It's my birthday, why can't I do what I want?" The next thing I knew, my father grabbed me around the waist, put his hand over my mouth, and hauled me out the door and into the car, kicking and screaming. I don't remember what happened after that, but I guess my brother and mother followed us out, because they were in the car when we got home.

I woke up the next day eyes all puffy from crying, and I had a headache. Nobody talked to me at breakfast. I went right back to my room and stayed there all day. Three things changed after that. I knew I'd never miss another birthday party. I knew the drawing pad and colored crayolas in the square package weren't worth it. And I knew Grandpa ruled.

The Wringer

The Wringer

Curiosity. It's delicious and dangerous. I always thought it was delicious, like anticipating the taste of vanilla ice cream covered with chunks of chocolate candy. My mother was the one who said it was dangerous. Every time she'd say that, I'd always giggle. It made her mad, but I couldn't help it. I couldn't see how being curious hurt anything. Until the wringer.

A wringer was a metal frame with rollers connected to old-time washing machines. People filled the washer tub with water, poured in the soap and turned on the machine. It swished the clothes around and around until they were clean. My brother used to stand on a little stool next to the washer and watch as his blanket went under and up and around. When he couldn't see it, his face would get all squinched up.

There was no "spin cycle." When the clothes were done, Mom fed each piece separately through the wringer. The ringer had two rollers that looked a lot like the tubes left over from Christmas wrapping. The rollers were covered in a spongy kind of material. A spring attached to the frame adjusted how close the rollers were pressed together. If you were wringing my socks, it had to be tighter than if you were wringing a heavy towel. You pushed the sock into the place where the two rollers come together and then turned the handle. The sock went through the two rollers and the water got pushed back into the tub. The sock dropped into a basket, ready to be hung outside on the clothesline. The operation was repeated for every piece.

Then someone invented a motor driven wringer. You just put the sock between the rollers, pressed a button, and zoom, the motor sucked in the sock, squished out all the water and dropped it in the basket like magic. Mom didn't have one of those. But my friend's mom had just gotten one. So, of course, I was curious.

My friend and I were supposed to be coloring, but when her mom went outside to water plants, we snuck into the basement to test the new invention. We wet two socks. When it was time to push the button, my friend didn't want to get in trouble, so she wouldn't do it. I made some remark like, "You're such a scaredy cat", grabbed the sock, stuck it in the wringer and pushed the button. Like magic, it sucked in the sock, squished it and delivered it into the basket waiting below. But the motor didn't stop. It kept making the rollers go around and around. So I stuck in the second sock—only that time, the rollers not only got the sock but my right arm, too. Like a horror movie, there I was with the wringer sucking in my arm, further and further, up past the wrist. It sucked its way to my elbow. Certain it would suck in my whole body, kill me and deliver me into the basket. I let out a blood-curdling yell.

My friend ran for her mother. By then, the rollers sucked in my elbow and were pinching the dickens out of my armpit. Tears streamed down my face. All I could think of was my mother saying, "Curiosity can be dangerous." Shame and terror overcame me by the time her mother pulled the plug.

She didn't say one word. She gave me one of those "looks" and called my mother. That night, my father inflicted 10 swats on my bottom with his fraternity paddle. My arm had black and blue wringer marks for weeks. But mostly I had a new respect for the word "curiosity."

The Green Bike

The Green Bike

Riding my bike, wind whipping my hair and whistling in my ears, super! We lived on a large hill. There were no busy streets, so I was allowed to ride my bike anywhere, as long as I didn't go too fast. But I liked fast. There were no driveways or intersections, so what could happen?

I couldn't ride up the steep hill. I had to push the bike. But I never tired of going down, even though it meant having to push up afterwards. Mounting my bike at the top, I was an Amazon princess, tall and powerful.

Then came "the bad day." As usual, I pulled my green bike out of the garage, walked it to the end of the drive, and headed down. It was cold. My arms chilled right through my turtleneck. But it felt wonderful on my face, like little pinpricks of excitement. It was Saturday morning, and I had been waiting hours to be allowed out. Mom said, "Wait until it gets warmer."

Down the hill I went, feet poised on the brakes, pigtails standing out in back like broken antennae. I wasn't going any faster than usual, but because of the cold air, it felt faster, so I hit the brakes. Nothing happened. The front wheel slid sideways. I turned the handlebars to change direction. The end whipped around. I hit the brakes again. Still nothing. The more I turned, the more I skidded the wrong way. Everything spun. Then everything went black.

The next thing I remember was sitting in my brother's red wagon. My father pulled the wagon up the hill with a neighbor pushing behind. My knee was bleeding buckets. My mother cried like a lawn sprinkler and tried to hold my knee together. Then everything went black again.

When I woke up the second time I was in the hospital. My knee was covered in a huge, white bandage like you see in old war movies. My mother wasn't crying anymore. She looked mad. My dad didn't say anything. That's what he did when he was really, really angry. He just gave you that "look." Nobody knows what happened. I just remember spinning and yelling. Mom heard me from the shower and came running with wet hair and in her bathrobe. All the neighbors saw her. She never forgave me.

One neighbor said the road was still in the shade and slick from the cold night before. I'm glad I don't remember the crash. I missed four days of school and still have a scar on my knee.

My beautiful green bike lay mangled in the garage until dad donated it to a bike shop for parts. All summer I walked while my friends rode. For my October birthday, I prayed for a new bike. No bike. Finally, a sparkling red and black bike rolled up next to the Christmas tree. Mom thought I'd be scared to ride. I wasn't. I had learned caution the hard way.

Giraffes

In third grade, I went to a private school where they taught world geography, about places like Africa, China and Australia. Now, kids see those countries on TV, but then there were no such things as the Discovery Channel or Animal Planet.

We studied pictures of strangely shaped animals like elephants, giraffes, kangaroos and duck-billed platypuses. People from Africa and China looked different from any people I'd ever seen. And Australia looked as if nothing could live there at all, but things did. I wanted to know everything about everywhere, and I wanted to go to all those places someday.

I especially liked those big, tall animals with the long necks and the big eyes—giraffes. I wanted to see how they really looked and walked and ate stuff off trees. And how did they ever get down low enough to drink from a pond? And wouldn't it be wonderful to be taller than anyone?

I begged my parents to take me to the Bronx Zoo. Mom said I had to learn a lot about giraffes before she'd take me. We went to the library and checked out three big reference books. I found out that giraffes are six feet tall when they're born. Giraffes also fall six feet to the ground during birth and land on their heads. I tried to think what would have happened to my baby brother if he fell on this head at birth. Not a pretty thought.

Giraffes have only seven bones in their necks, same as us. Some of those bones must be pretty long. Their tongues are 22 inches long and black at the end to protect them from the sun. The spots on a giraffe are like fingerprints. No two are exactly alike. Finally, Mom was satisfied and we scheduled a trip.

The zoo was magic. Everything was strange and exotic--tigers, lions, mountain goats, elephants and hippos. The two I remember best were the polar bears and the giraffes. The polar bears were all white and gigantic. They lumbered around the enclosure like huge, moving buildings.

I expected the ground to shake each time their paws, bigger than most of my body, hit the ground. With all that weight, they swam so easily, their white fur fanning out like puffballs in the water!

The giraffes made me gasp. They were so tall. The male was almost 20 feet, as tall as the second floor of our house. When the daddy giraffe came up close, it took a long time for me to look from his black hoofs all the way up to the top of his head. He had round, black eyes and eyelashes at least as long as my hand. I tried to memorize his spots so I could compare them to the females and double-check my research.

The female, slightly smaller than the male, sauntered over, followed by two adorable baby giraffes. The tall youngsters surveyed us with some curiosity until their mother nudged them as if to say, "Be careful babies." The four stood motionless, yellow skyscrapers gazing down at us. The male yawned and his immense tongue flapped around like an escaping snake.

Just then, the zookeeper opened a gate at the other end and the family turned abruptly, loping toward anticipated food. Their tall bodies flowed in graceful strides, long necks arching as they galloped. "They're going 100 miles an hour," I said to Mom. But I knew from my research that about 30 miles per hour was their limit. For weeks, I dreamed of giraffes and of going to Africa.

Silver Beach

Silver Beach

On holidays, we sometimes went to Little Grandma's beach house. I told my friends it was in Frog's Neck. Wrong, it was Throgs Neck. I still don't know what a Throgs Neck is. We went there even before I could remember anything. I know that because I've seen pictures of us on the deck that stuck out from the side of a hill and overlooked the beach.

Any time of the day, you could look over the railing around the deck and see people and dogs walking along the water. To get from Grandma's to the beach, we had to walk a long way down a narrow, pebbled path then open a gate. Lots of steps led to the beach. Going down took forever when you were hot and carrying pails and shovels and a radio. Coming up was worse. From the bottom, those steps looked like the highest hill on a roller coaster. Even Grandpa didn't like it. He used to stop two or three times going up to catch his breath. I was always glad he stopped because I needed to rest, too, but I didn't want to be a sissy, so I never said anything.

Silver Beach was mysterious. Narrow gravel walking paths went all along the hill, and you never knew where you'd end up. Trees grew intertwined with each other. It was great for hide and seek and endless giggles from behind root branches. If you walked far enough along the gravel path past the gate to the beach, you got to houses big as hotels. Going the opposite way on the pebbled path brought us to the village square.

The ice cream parlor was my favorite place. Other shops crowded around a bricked open square, but all I remember were the steps up to the ice cream store. It was dark inside. Metal tables and chairs with fancy wrought iron decoration were scattered around on the marble floor. A long counter with high stools, always full of big kids, went along one wall. Tin milk shake containers lined the shelves, along with sundae dishes and banana split plates. A display case filled with candies and pastry made parents say, "I can't resist. They look so delicious."

Grandpa usually took us to the ice cream parlor. I always wanted two scoops, but most of the time I only got to have one. Rocky road hadn't been invented yet, so I got chocolate or coconut. Grandpa always got two scoops, even though Grandma told him he should only have one. My brother always wanted a banana split, but most of the time he settled for vanilla. On the Fourth of July, Grandpa would take us to the ice cream parlor, get us two scoops, then rent a two-peopled bike in the square and take us for rides.

We never stayed at Silver Beach long enough. Maybe that's why it remained mysterious. Exploring always turned up some new flower or bug or a scary adult coming through the trees when we were trying to hide. And sitting on the deck in the sun, looking at the beach and the water, made me feel free. I often wonder if Silver Beach still exists and, if it does, who lives in Grandma's house.

Buster

Buster

Buster was my best friend at Silver Beach. His Grandmother lived down the pebbled path from my Little Grandma. Buster was his nickname. I don't remember his real name. It was very long and hard to pronounce. His Grandfather came from Russia. Understanding Buster's grandfather was hard, except when he was mad. Then "No" and "Go Home" came out very clearly. Buster's Grandmother wasn't from Russia, so I could understand her. She made hot chocolate for us.

Our favorite game was hide-and-seek. With all the bushes, rocks and enclosed decks, there were plenty of places to hide. Sometimes it would take Buster almost eight minutes to find me. I always found him in less than five minutes. But Buster never got mad. Sometimes I'd try to make him mad just to see what he'd look like angry, but he never got mad. When we were tired, we played checkers. Most of the time, he won.

Buster stayed with his grandparents for a month each summer. But one summer he didn't come. I asked my Little Grandma, "Where's Buster?" She looked sad and said he was sick. I tried to get her to tell me what he had—chicken pox, the flu, measles—but she wouldn't say. She'd just sigh and act sad. When she looked that way, I felt scared. Little Grandma said the grandparents had gone to Buster's house in Connecticut to help.

Finally, Little Grandma said, "Buster will be here tomorrow." I was so excited. "Don't get too excited," she said. "Buster has been very sick. He won't be able to play." I didn't care. I just wanted to see Buster. I could hardly sleep all night, planning the new places I'd hide. The next morning, I sat on a rock in front of our house and waited.

At last, the black station wagon with the tan wood on the sides came rumbling down the road. Buster's grandpa got out and went to the back seat. I started to run toward the car, but he stopped me with a glare. He reached into the back seat and lifted Buster out of the car. Buster's legs dangled like the pigtails on Raggedy Ann. Buster looked at me and then looked away. He didn't even say, "Hello." Buster's father took a big, metal chair out of the back. It had huge wheels on each side. They put Buster in the chair and wheeled him into the house.

"We didn't know how to tell you," said Little Grandma. "Buster has polio. You can't go over there because you might catch it. He's been in an iron lung and may never walk again."

"What's polio," I asked. But nobody seemed very sure. Every day I looked over at the house. Sometimes they would put Buster on the deck. I knew a secret path through the woods. I'd sneak around the path and look at Buster, but I didn't want to catch something that would make my legs go like pigtails on Raggedy Ann, so I didn't get too close.

Finally, Buster's grandmother came over and said the danger had passed. I ran over as quick as I could. Buster didn't want to talk. So I went and got the checkers. He beat me four times before he said a single word. Then he told me how scared he'd been in the hospital, how they'd kept him in an iron cage that helped him breathe, and how he was still scared.

I told Buster I'd missed him terribly and that even if he couldn't walk, we could still play checkers and cards. He grinned. We played lots of cards and checkers that summer.

Buster's grandfather died that fall. The family sold their summer home at Silver Beach. I heard that Buster learned to walk with crutches, but I never saw my friend again after he went back to Connecticut.

The
Hill
House

The Hill House

Our best house was at the tippy top of a huge hill in Mt. Kisco, New York. When it snowed, my dad couldn't drive up. He had to park the car at the bottom, and walk up. He panted like a dog when he came in, and nobody could talk to him for a few minutes. The hill house had a wonderful yard—lots of grass, a great wooden fence to climb, hills to run over, and two huge trees.

Dad hung a swing on the biggest tree. It was two strands of very large rope stuck through the holes in a fat, flat board. Dad climbed high into the tree to hang the ropes. He said if I ever climbed up there, I'd get a whopping. On the swing, if you pumped hard enough, you could see high over the ridge and down to where the road went. At the top of the swing cycle a little jerk happened, and it felt like falling down a fast elevator, your lunch pushing up into your throat.

Lew and I had great fun in the yard. We wanted to swing every day. But when it rained, the place where our feet touched the ground got all gooey and full of mud, so we weren't allowed. But on cold winter days, we'd swing until our noses resembled "Rudolph" and our fingers froze to the ropes. After peeling off the swing, we'd tumble down the snowy hill and make angels at the bottom.

On hot summer days, the swing provided a caressing breeze and the smell of wildflowers along the hill. Then the bumpy yard became our obstacle course. While Mom was folding laundry in the basement, I'd drag the hose to the top of the hill, point it downward, put a rock on top to hold it, run down to the house and turn on the water full blast. Then we'd wait. At first, nothing happened. But after a few minutes, little rivers gushed all over from the top of the hill, running in and out the bumps, down the rocks behind the garage, across the patio and all the way to the mailbox.

Lew and I watched the magic. It wasn't a backyard anymore. It was streams rushing into rivers, carrying trees and rocks to the ocean. It was mountains and crags and shimmering lakes.

The water made rippling sounds and dug curvy ditches down the hill and around the humps. It never sloshed in a straight line. We'd put rocks and sticks in the way to change the direction. When it got too close to the swing, where it might make gooey mud, we'd turn it off. Then we'd take turns swinging while we waited for our magic aqua-environment to disappear.

Making rivers occupied many sunny afternoons, until Mom discovered us throwing rocks into a particularly gushing crack next to a particularly high mound. Dad had wondered why mowing the lawn got harder and harder. Mom screamed at the sight and turned into 'motorized-mom,' running to shut off the water. I got in a lot of trouble. She put me in my room with no supper.

Maybe that's why we moved. Or maybe my dad got tired of walking up the hill in winter and mowing the grass in summer.

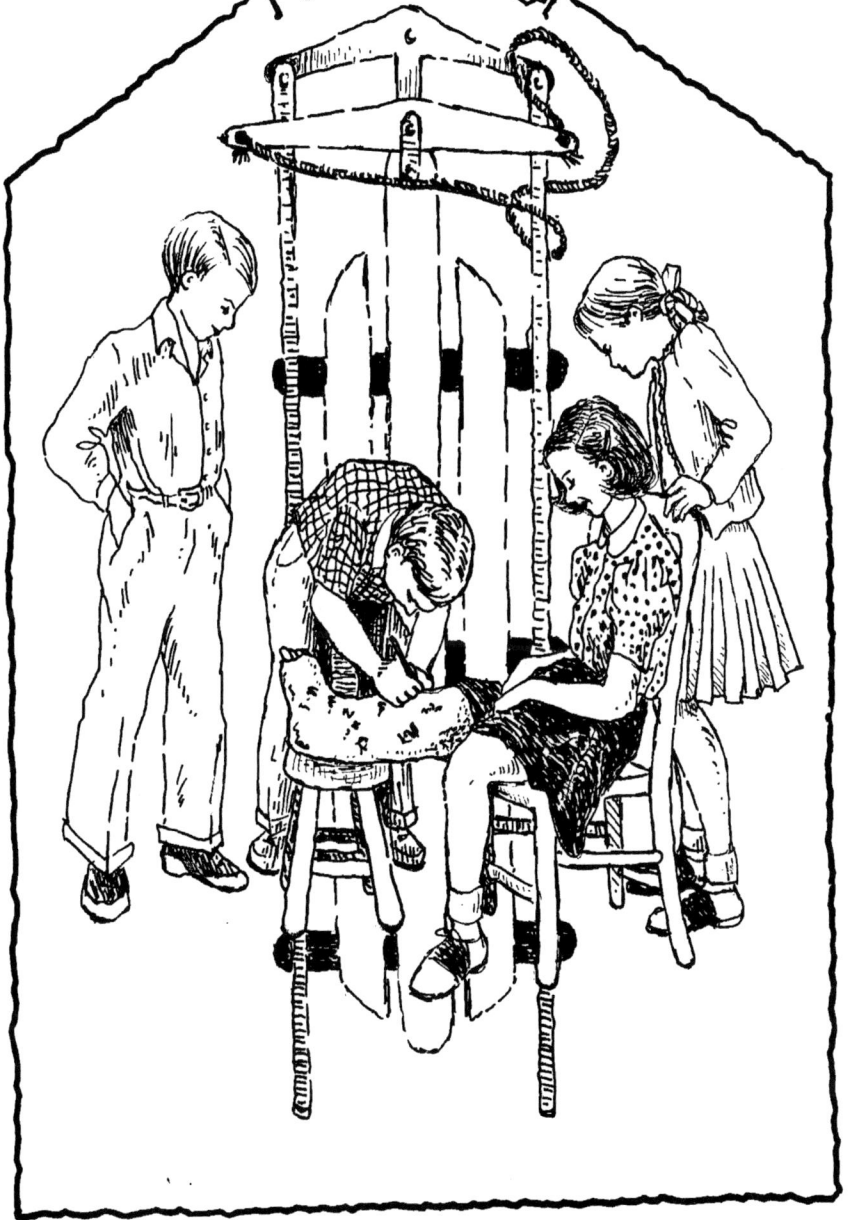

The Sled

The Sled

The first snow came in early November. As soon as it piled as high as our index finger stuck down into it, we were allowed to grab our sleds and ride down the hill beside the house. Mom always reminded us, "Don't get off the hill and sled down the road, you might run into a car."

One morning, Judy, who lived across the street, decided to sled down the road to the bus stop because she was late. Going down the road was faster than the hill. She planned to hide her sled behind a bush and retrieve it after school. We were all at the bus stop, waiting and wondering if she was sick and not coming to school. Then we saw her flip her sled onto the road. The slushy snow from the day before had frozen. Just as she hopped on the sled, the school bus scrunched around the corner and screeched to a stop at the bottom of the hill.

Five of us, all bundled up in our mittens, jackets and snow boots hollered, "Stop" but she couldn't stop. The snow had turned to ice and down she came, faster and faster and faster. We waved our arms and leaped like jumping beans. She paid no attention.

The next ten seconds crept by in slow motion. Judy screamed, "Help, Help, Help." She tried steering the sled off the road, but nothing happened. It just came faster and faster. Finally, one of the older girls yelled, "Jump!" She did. A second later the sled rammed into the tire of the bus. Pieces of wood flew everywhere. One even cracked a window on the bus. The sled's metal handles wedged themselves around the bus tire. The yellow paint all around the bus wheel was scratched, and pieces of sled dotted the dirty snow like pepper.

Judy lay in a crumpled pile on the side of the road, crying. The bus driver leaped out of the bus. He knew something was broken because her left foot faced a different direction than her right. He covered her with a blanket, tried to get her to stop crying, and called for help on the bus radio. We were told, "Get on the bus and be quiet!"

Shortly after, Judy's mom ran down the hill crying and yelling, "Oh, my God, my baby!" An ambulance came up the hill, skidding on the ice. Red lights and radios blared. Still, all of us had to sit still and not ask any questions. It was cold in the bus, and we were all scared. One friend cried so hard they had to send her home.

Finally, they took Judy away in the ambulance. We thought maybe she'd die. The bus driver said, "No, she's not dead, just a little broken." We were really late for school that day. They had to send another bus because of the sled wrapped around the wheel. When we finally did get to school, we couldn't concentrate, let alone spell. The loudspeaker finally announced that Judy had broken a leg, sprained her shoulder, and had lots of bruises.

When she came back to school, Judy had a cast almost to her hip and couldn't even walk. After a month, the casts began to get smaller. She could walk with crutches. Finally, she walked right on the cast. She had a cast on her leg for

Christmas, for Valentine's Day, and clear until Easter.

Judy's mother and my mom had lots of ammunition for lectures about not taking sleds on the street. The fun part was signing our names on all Judy's different casts.

The Hiding Place

The Hiding Place

My first hiding place was half a block from my house in a clump of trees. I used to go there when the house was too noisy, or too quiet, or too anything I didn't like. I wasn't really hiding, just thinking. It felt good, feeling the breeze blow the leaves and making them talk like girls whispering behind the teacher's back. October was best. The leaves turned yellow and red and orange. They made crunching sounds under my feet as they fell.

After the leaves fell off, it wasn't a good hiding place. My mother saw me there. She asked me what I was doing. I said, "Nothing, just sitting."

She looked at me for a long time then said, "Just sitting?"

"Yes," I said, "just sitting."

"Are you sad?" she asked?

"No," I said, because I wasn't.

"Are you angry?" she asked.

"No," I said, because I wasn't. She just sort of huffed and went home. That night, Dad and Mom got together and told me not to go there any more. They said it wasn't safe. I missed my hiding place.

How could I find another hiding place, one that was safe? It had to be outside—or close to outside, anyway. The sun had to come in, and the snow had to stay out. All winter I scouted for a new hiding place. My eyes searched the snow banks, the back of the garage, the basement. None of them were right.

Finally, I found the perfect place, right in my own back yard. It was the garden shed. Nobody ever went in there, except my dad on Saturday mornings when he had to cut the grass or clip the bushes. It was home to a huge assortment of awkward looking tools--rakes, shovels, things that looked like shovels only smaller and with claws, several sizes of empty buckets, and lots of buckets half full of paint or stain or other bad smelling stuff. Oh, and a huge box full of brushes, rollers and paint sticks.

When I wanted to be alone, I would go out to the garden shed, leaving the door open two foot-lengths so the light would sprinkle over the buckets and paint cans. Then I'd take one of the big, empty buckets and turn it upside down and sit on it. Sometimes I would bring a book, and I could take as long as I wanted to read one page. Other times I just sat making patterns in the dirt with my feet and thinking about stuff. It wasn't as pretty as the tree place, but nobody bothered me there.

I had to find new hiding places lots of times because we moved a lot. There was always a hiding place somewhere. One time it was the corner of a laundry room where someone had started building a bathroom, got one wall erected, and stopped. Another time it was an old chair my Dad always meant to discard, but it sat in the garage. Nobody could see me because the chair faced the wall. Once it was the inside of a broken-down horse trailer belonging to the grumpy next-door neighbor. It smelled like a mixture of hay and horse poop.

When I got bigger, I didn't use my hiding places as much. But I always had one. There was always a place I could go when the house got too noisy, or too quiet, or too whatever I didn't like.

My Fourth Grade Teacher

My 4th Grade Teacher

Fourth grade made me persistent. I loved reading stories by myself. Every time I got 100% on multiplication, I felt so smart. I wrote stories as fast as I could think up strange people, strange animals, and stranger places to explore. But I hated Mrs. Brown, my fourth grade teacher.

My other teachers had been fine.

My kindergarten teacher, Mrs. H (H was for Horowitz, which none of us could say or spell), laughed a lot and sang songs. She made us work really hard at counting to 100 and sounding out words.

My first grade teachers—three of them because we moved a lot—I don't remember.

My second grade teacher frowned, but she was nice. She let us act in skits and we pretended to be people from history like George Washington or Patrick Henry.

In third grade, my teacher made us walk like soldiers and hold hands at the door. Once a week someone got to be the line leader. Usually it was a boy, but I got to do it twice.

Then there was Mrs. Brown's fourth grade.

She didn't like me because I was a tomboy. I climbed on everything and sat on the floor with my legs crossed. I liked to sit at my desk and put my left foot over my right knee. It was comfortable. But in those days, girls had to wear dresses. No pants were allowed. Every time she'd see me with my leg crossed under my skirt, she'd hustle over, ruler in hand, smack me on the knee and say, "Penny, act like a lady!"

She glared at me, her green eyes spitting fire. She just stood there glaring. When she got like that, her curly red hair would seem even redder. I wondered if those curls wouldn't turn into hissing snakes and bite me all over. I always obeyed, but inside, I was angry. Why didn't she leave me alone?

She tried to make me write with my right hand, too. I'd been left-handed since way before first grade. I could write my name, PENNY ALBRIGHT, before I started kindergarten. My kindergarten teacher, Mrs. H., tried to make me right-handed, but when it didn't work she put me at a table where I could write without turning my hand upside down. But Mrs. Brown with the red hair never gave up. Day after day after day she tried to make me right-handed. Every day, I fumed at Mrs. Brown for bopping me on the leg and trying to make me change hands.

Finally, one day I got really mad. When I got mad, I yelled or cried. That day I did both at the same time. I yelled, "I don't have to write with my right hand and I'm not going to." Then I started crying. She sent me to the principal.

My mother had to come to school—and my father, too. They made me stay home for two days. Then I had to apologize to Mrs. Brown for being rude. But the next week I had a different class and a teacher who didn't make me change my writing hand or hit me on the knee.

The Suburbs

New House in the Suburbs

We lived in lots of places close to New York City. But the place we lived longest was "Carl Place" on Long Island. It was something new, called a "Subdivision." All the houses were new and built in neat little rows. All were two stories and square, like a big cereal box or a short half-gallon milk carton. Some had three windows on the front, others had four. Some had a porch. Others had a small stoop. All had a very narrow walkway from the front door to the street. Next to the walkway stood a mailbox. Every mailbox was painted white and looked exactly the same as every other mailbox, except for the numbers.

"These new developments are springing up like weeds," said Mom. She didn't much like the way everything looked the same. So she developed an elaborate plan for the yard to make ours look different. There would be little hills, places for flowers, decorative rock, and a playhouse—but grass would dominate.

We moved into the house in November. It snowed the day after we moved. It snowed almost every day until March. When it got warm enough, the snow and ice melted into mud—sticky, gooey, brown, staining mud. Soon, brown mud covered the step, the front hall, the carpet, the kitchen, the garage, and the bathroom. Mom cried; her new house was ruined.

Dad went to the hardware store, bought two foot-scrapers, and threatened us with grounding if we brought in mud. It was hard keeping on the sidewalk from the front door to the street. If you turned around quickly to get something you forgot, you fell off into the mud. If you were talking and not watching your feet, you fell in the mud. It was even harder when kids came over with everyone laughing, talking and walking all at the same time. Mom put two big shaggy rugs next to the door and instructed us to remove our shoes as soon as we entered.

By May, the mud had receded and all the dads spent lots of time in their identical lots trying to grow grass. Not at our house. My mother became

"Police Officer Mom," directing traffic about the yard, consulting her drawings, and sending my father with the wheelbarrow or me with a cart to wherever her chart called for hills or rocks. Even Lew had to load up his pail with colored pebbles. My father hauled the rocks and stones in the wheelbarrow. It was my job to carry extra dirt and deposit it within the borders of a soon-to-be flower garden. Why do we have to be different, I thought? Our neighbors were planting plain, flat grass. Their daughter rode her bike instead of hauling dirt.

Dad laid bricks in a circle and Mom planted orange and yellow flowers. Dad laid bricks along the driveway and Mom planted forsythia bushes. Dad arranged rocks in a pile and Mom sprinkled wildflower seeds. Dad rented a digger with a big wheel that turned over the mud clods and smoothed out the yard. Mom, Lew and I sprinkled grass seed. Then "Police Officer Mom" ordered us, "Stay off the lawn. Don't walk, jump, fall or tiptoe."

She watered the flowers and the dirt every day. By July we had hills, grass, a decorative rock pile full of wildflowers, three flowerbeds full of orange and yellow blossoms, and a driveway resembling a formal garden entry. Mom made Dad paint the mailbox green, and she applied floral stickers. Even though the playhouse had to wait, Mom was happy. Other moms in the subdivision would stop by to compliment her on "such an unusual and lovely" yard. She'd smile and say, "The whole family helped."

Aunt Gertie's House

Uncle Ernest & Aunt Gertie - "Big" G'ma + Grandpa

Connie

Lew

Victor, Carl Robert, Penny

Christmas at Aunt Gertie's

Christmas at Aunt Gertie's

Just getting to Auntie Gertie's for Christmas was an adventure. First we folded down the back seat in the station wagon. Then we put down an old sheet. We carried out all the wrapped Christmas packages. Even Lew carried ones that weren't breakable. Dad packed. He put the big boxes at the bottom, the smaller ones on top with old towels stuck between them. Odd sized gifts were squeezed between the others. Sometimes we had so many I had to sit in the middle of the seat so Dad could pile more next to the door. I didn't like that much because then I couldn't see when we crossed the bridges.

There were two bridges. One was really, really high, like being at the top of a Ferris wheel in a car. It had lots of cables reaching from the platforms to the highway. One Christmas, the wind whipped our car. As we got to the middle of the bridge, it felt like a swing. The car kept going straight, but it felt sideways too. Mom said it made her nauseous.

The other bridge had big steel beams that hid the boats below. Just as I'd sight a sailboat, whissh, a beam would be in the way. I'd see the white sail for a second and another beam would whissh by. After the bridges, we drove down a narrow street and came to a hilly area with lots of brick houses.

Auntie's house had three floors, an attic, and the gigantic basement where we all had Christmas Dinner. Sometimes more than 30 people came for dinner. We always had turkey and stuffing and ham and three different pies for dessert. Uncle Earnest always said grace standing at the head of the table. If anybody squirmed or talked during grace, he had to start over. One time, my cousin Carl Robert, who liked to talk as much as I did, made Uncle Earnest start over three times.

Carl Robert was my favorite. He and I loved to run up and down the stairs from floor to floor and play hide and seek. Some of the others played too, but Carl Robert and I always found the best hiding places. When nobody was looking, we went all the way to the attic, lay on the bed, and looked at the peak in the roof and the lines in the wood. We made up stories about the lines in the wood as if they were streets going to strange and exciting places that we'd visit together some day.

The only one who could always find us was Cousin Connie. She always knew what we were doing and where to find us. She was older and knew lots more about everything. She tried to explain that Auntie Gertie was really our grandmother's sister, so she wasn't really our aunt and that we weren't really cousins, either—but Carl Robert and I didn't care.

Connie's little brother, Buzz (his real name was Victor), always wanted to go with us, but he was younger and we wanted nothing to do with him or Lew or Carl Robert's little brother, Wick. So we made a game of getting away from them and finding places where we could be alone.

At Christmas, all the children got two gifts. After the gifts, we sang a song or recited something we memorized. One year I said the whole "Night Before Christmas" by memory. Another time, Lew and I and Buzz sang "Jingle Bells" and tried to move our hands in a pattern like singers in a quartet. Instead, we bumped hands and Lew hit Buzz in the face and Buzz got mad and said naughty words, and if Connie hadn't saved us we'd all have been in the cellar facing the wall on stiff chairs. That's what happened to Lew and Buzz once when they tried to flush one of Auntie's red, high-heeled shoes down the toilet.

After dinner and the entertainment, the adults drank coffee and talked about stuff. You could hear the white china cups clicking against the saucers. Sometimes the women would giggle and then talk really quiet. When the men went into the den and turned on the radio, then the kids got to play with toys. Connie would help the younger ones, but Carl Robert and I liked to steal their toys and play with them ourselves. We knew we were naughty, but we didn't care.

Time-to-go arrived much too soon, and saying goodbye was dreadful. Everybody hugged and hugged and kissed and kissed and the grandmas all cried. We packed the car with a different assortment of gifts than we had brought, then we headed home. I often wished secretly that Connie, Carl Robert and I could hide away and live at Auntie Gertie's for a whole year. Then maybe she'd let us wind the huge grandfather clock that stood on the steps and gonged out the hours.

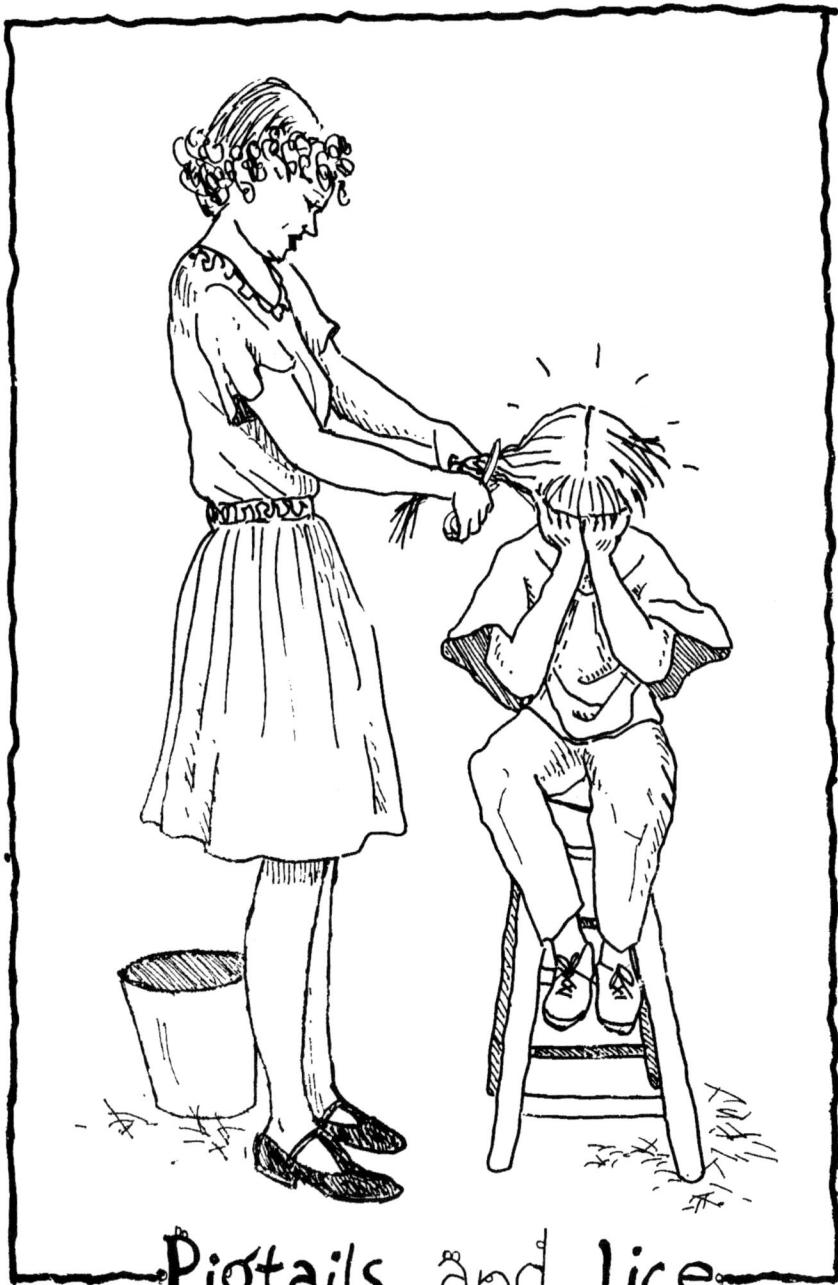

Pigtails and Lice

Pigtails and Lice

Our elementary school stood grandly on a grassy square right across the street from our "shoebox" house. A new school, built for a new subdivision, its polished red bricks stretched two stories high. All the kids in the neighborhood attended that school and usually gathered there on Saturdays to play.

The howls of laughter and an occasional "You're cheating" were disturbed only by warnings from mothers who clustered on nearby benches, sharing whatever young mothers talk about. One Saturday, children of varying ages played baseball, tag or jump-rope. Some roughness occurred, and an occasional tear dripped down a sad face, but the warm spring air made it hard to be glum.

Then, two days after the wonderful Saturday, every student was given a sealed envelope to carry home. The envelopes had big, yellowish-orange alert signs at the top. My mother read the notice with alarm. She made a little humphing sound, took me to the bathroom against my wishes, and began examining my head.

My hair had never been cut. It hung past my waist in two long pigtails, the braiding of which gave my mother much pride. Sometimes she wound them around my head like a crown. Other times, huge bows of various colors were attached at the ends. She pulled and prodded at my head. Finally, she said, "You're OK, you don't have any."

"Any what?" I asked.

"Lice," she answered with her face all contorted as if she'd just swallowed a whole lemon. Lice. I had no idea what they were or did. So, I asked lots of questions. I was famous for that. I found out lice are some kind of little head bug that you catch from other children who've caught them from other children who are dirty. They multiply really fast, and you can't go back to school until you're rid of them 100%.

The following Monday, the school nurse came into our class and examined all the girls. She pulled on my braids, unbraided the hair and pulled up until I could feel my bottom coming off the chair. She shot a worried look at my teacher and left. My mother arrived looking like she did when my brother had a potty accident, and I had to go home. I had lice. I wanted to know who in my class wasn't clean, but I couldn't figure it out.

"You should have her head shaved, you know," the doctor said after busting into the room hurriedly. My mother started crying. I didn't know what head shaving was, so I just sat there. I'd never seen my mother beg before, but she begged the doctor for my hair. Finally, he agreed that a short bob would do if she'd comb it daily with a baby-fine comb and wash with some disgusting smelling soap.

That night, I sat in the chair and watched my two beautifully braided pigtails fall to the floor like dead snakes. If I hadn't been scared to death of the lice, I would have protested. I cried for the whole two weeks I had to stay home from school. Once in a while, Mom cried with me. She even got out a picture of me with hair and assured me it would grow back.

The morning I returned to school I was so embarrassed. I shrank two inches as I approached the classroom. Then I saw two of my best girlfriends. They both had short hair, too.

The War

The War

My dad had never talked to me like a grown-up before. Then one night, he sat me on the big couch next to his big chair. He talked to me in the tone of voice I'd heard him use with Mom when he was worried. He talked about war. He said some countries were "bullies" like that nasty Michael who lived down the street. Sometimes countries had to defend themselves, just like a kid has to stand up to a bully. He talked about defending our country and about his friend Jim, who had died in Hawaii when the war started several years ago.

I didn't really understand the word "war." I did know that some people called "Japs," who didn't look like us, attacked people who did look like us and killed a lot of them in a place called Hawaii, far away over another ocean. After that, our country started fighting back. They were also fighting another bully called Germany, where people called "Nazis" lived. Those people were bullying our friends France and England.

After our talk about war, Dad went to meetings two nights a week and helped plan how to protect us from bombs. Then came the "blackouts." We pulled black shades down over all the windows and turned off all the lights. Mom said it was because we lived near a shipping port, and the Germans would know where to bomb ships carrying ammunition if they could see the lights. Old Mr. Osborne, our neighbor, was the air-raid warden. He walked around the neighborhood to make sure everything was dark. If he saw light anywhere, he could give us a ticket.

I was allowed to have a small flashlight in my bed, where I could read books. "But don't shine it out the window," warned my father. I never shined it out the window, but sometimes I had to peek out to see if I could see any Nazi planes. I'd watch all the lights of the city go out one by one until it was pitch dark. There were no cars moving, no people walking and talking as they passed by, no traffic or radios, just quiet. I'd peek out, search the sky, and listen. I wondered what it would be like for a kid in England, where bombs had already knocked down houses and bridges.

The worst part of the air-raid drills was the noise. The air-raid siren started kind of low and whiney. It got louder and louder, until the sound blasted and screamed. It whined and screamed for a long time. Then, slowly, it unwound—like a person whistling and running out of breath. My brother hated that siren and screamed bloody murder. Mom would put him in his bed and lay beside him. He'd holler and put the pillow over his face until the siren wound down.

When we visited Grandma at Silver Beach, it was even worse. There was no siren, but they had a warden who came around blowing a shrill whistle. And they had blackouts and a curfew every night. Everyone had to be inside with the lights off by 8 o'clock. If the warden spotted even the littlest shaft of light, he could arrest you. Grandma said that was because they were on the Indian River, and the tankers and ammunition barges were targets.

Other than the blackouts and the air raid drills, the war didn't mean much to us kids. Mom complained about making oleo. It was white, oozy and ugly, and it replaced butter. To make it look more like butter, you had to mix a little packet of orange coloring in with the goo and squeeze it like mad for a long time. We also had to take a book of coupons whenever we went to the store. We could only get one package of some things. Sometimes we couldn't buy sugar, even though the store had some. Meat was for special occasions.

The next time my dad talked to me in that adult tone of voice was when my friend Patty's mother came over to tell us Patty's dad, a Lieutenant in the U.S. army, had been killed fighting in Poland. My dad cried. My mom cried. Patty's mother and Patty and Patty's two brothers cried. Patty said her dad died defending his country and would get a medal. Dad said war was a terrible thing because lots of fathers on both sides had to die before it ended.

We went to the funeral. We had to get dressed in our best clothes and listen to lots of talking about how brave Patty's father had been. Then we were supposed to walk by this big box that had her daddy's body in it and an American flag over the top. I didn't want to walk up there, and I didn't want look at that box. But Dad jerked me by the arm and made me go. I squinched up my eyes until they were almost closed and walked by that box as fast as Dad's hand would let me.

The next day, Patty's mother put a small flag in the window. It was red around the outside, white in the center and had one gold star in the middle. The gold star told everyone in the community that the family living in the house had lost someone in the war. Friends stopped by with meat loaf or flowers or groceries. The minister came to Patty's almost every day.

Patty cried at every little thing. Mom said, "Be nice to Patty. She misses her daddy." When the next school year started, Patty's family moved in with her grandmother in Connecticut.

The Forest Fire

The Forest Fire

Our station wagon, stuffed with clothes, toys, food, and everything we'd need for a month, bumped over the rutted road and arrived at "Barnegat Pines." It vibrated green. The cabin we'd rented came straight out of "The Three Bears." Tumbling out, we unpacked and then charged to the top of the hill. Was the view as beautiful as the brochure claimed? Yes! Majestic pine trees stretched, spine-like, toward the sky in every direction. Dad had to go back to the city for four days before he could return.

But two days later, a forest ranger knocked at our door. Some careless campers hadn't properly put out their campfire. The wind came up, blew hard, and the embers ignited. A forest fire was moving toward us. "Don't go anywhere," he said. "Absolutely do not drive your car. You'll hear from us." By afternoon, the fire gobbled up trees at a ferocious speed. The forest crackled and smoked. The Forest Ranger told us to prepare for evacuation. We turned on the radio and waited.

The sky grayed with smoke. It smelled 15 times worse than grandpa's old ashtray. My eyes burned and itched like when I had the Chicken Pox, only worse. As night came, the sky turned an eerie pinkish-red color. We slept together with the radio beside us. In the morning, we climbed the hill behind our cabin. Smoke billowed higher than the clouds, and every few minutes red flames flashed upward with nasty snapping sounds. "We have to get ready," said Mom as we rushed back.

Soon after, an army truck arrived. You could hear the fire snapping and roaring in the distance. It sounded like a 100-car freight train rumbling and backfiring. It felt hotter than a sunburn at the beach. A soldier hurried us. The huge, greenish army truck, with wheels taller than me, squealed to a start after we tumbled in. There was no top. Rows of seats on each side were crammed with moms, dads, kids, and even a dog. The soldier said, "The fire's coming fast.

Get settled." His voice sounded urgent. Everyone, even the soldiers, looked scared.

The tank-like truck bumped and lunged through an area that had already burned. It stunk. The beautiful green trees were smoldering telephone poles. If I twisted my neck back and looked straight up, I could see little tufts of green at the very top. Everything else was black. Puffs of nasty smelling smoke came up from beneath the piles of burned needles.

The soldiers passed out bottles of water. They gave Lew and me a lollipop. Two more stops. The fire seemed further away. There were no more seats. We squealed to a halt in front of a tiny, sagging cabin. A very old man had to be lifted into the truck. Two other men left their seats to make room. They rode sitting on the front bumpers. The old lady across from me cried. She was saying some kind of prayer and fingering beads with a cross at the bottom. We made a turn. The men started talking. The soldier shouted, "quiet!" The lady didn't stop crying, but he didn't scold her. The only things you could hear were twigs snapping, crackling sounds, the motor of the big army truck, and the old lady crying.

Mom began talking quietly to the old lady and offered her a mint. I felt weak, as if my legs and arms wouldn't work. I thought of Buster. Lew's eyes were big as saucers. The old man had tears in his eyes and kept shaking his head up and down, up and down.

The truck crunched and snapped its way through the burnt forest. Nobody spoke until it lurched up onto a paved road. Then all the grownups cheered. Even the old man stopped shaking his head. We went to a high school gym, where they gave us peanut butter sandwiches and milk. About 80 people slept on the floor. The next day, my dad came for us.

Farm in Vermont

Farm in Vermont

The population of New York City drops a whole lot every summer. People escape to the mountains or the beach. Two of my school friends went to the Catskills with their mom. Their dad drove up on weekends. Mom's best friend went to Connecticut, and Mom's sister, Janet, went to Maine. Our neighbor went to the shore near Atlantic City. We went to my father's cousin's farm in Vermont for a week. The best thing about it? I got to see my favorite cousin, Carl Robert.

We crossed three bridges on our way out of New York. We passed skyscrapers that were so tall they blocked out the summer sun. After hours of passing houses, shopping centers, antique stores and apartments, we reached the country. Big, square fields of green bushes blended into flat, gold squares of something yellow that waved like my scarf on a cold windy day. Dad slowed down for a little town where he said they gave lots of traffic tickets. Then more flat, gold fields until we began climbing roller-coaster hills. The road snaked; the trees towered. I had to lean my head back so far to see the tops of the trees that I could have caught raindrops in my mouth. We swished past the sign that said, "Welcome to Vermont."

Cousin Connie's farm nestled into a hill surrounded by green fields and pastures fenced off into little squares. The farmhouse smelled of fresh coffee and vegetables. A kitchen table, covered with bright linoleum, was the gathering place for adults, who poured the first cup upon arrival and were still sipping steaming cups as we packed up to go home.

The worn barn, with its gray paint and smell of straw, was our favorite place. Plentiful hiding places made getting away from little brothers a simple game for Carl Robert and me. We climbed the loft ladder and hid behind bales of hay until the crybabies went to our moms and the moms made us include the younger brothers. My little brother was such a brat.

Carl Robert's brother, Wick, and my brother, Lew, loved "playing animals." It meant getting paper bags, string, colored paper and crayons. We made noses, tails, feathers and manes. When Carl Robert's friends visited, our farm parade included a horse, a cow, a pig, a goat, a chicken and a dog. When there were only four of us, we left out the goat and the dog.

Carl Robert was the cow because he was the boss, and that's what he wanted to be. I was supposed to be the horse because I was next biggest, and I loved horses. Wick had to be the chicken because he was the skinniest, and Carl Robert appointed Lew as the pig because he was chubbier than Wick.

But no! Lew wanted to be the horse. He wanted the mane and the bushy tail we'd made with yarn. He wouldn't play unless he could be the horse. If we didn't let him be the horse, he ran inside and told mom that we weren't sharing. Putting down her coffee cup and sighing, she'd say, "If he wants to be the horse, what difference does it make to you two grown-up kids, anyway?"

It was the way she said it. It made Carl Robert and me feel responsible for Lew being a brat. After that, every time we'd play animals, the same thing would happen. We'd prepare the costumes, Carl Robert would tell us what to be, and then Lew would throw a temper tantrum. First he'd yell. Then he'd stick out his tongue. He'd cry ferociously. He'd lay down on a bale of hay and kick. If none of that worked, he'd head toward the house to tell the moms. He always won. He ended up a horse, and I wore a stupid looking snout on my face and felt like a big, fat pig.

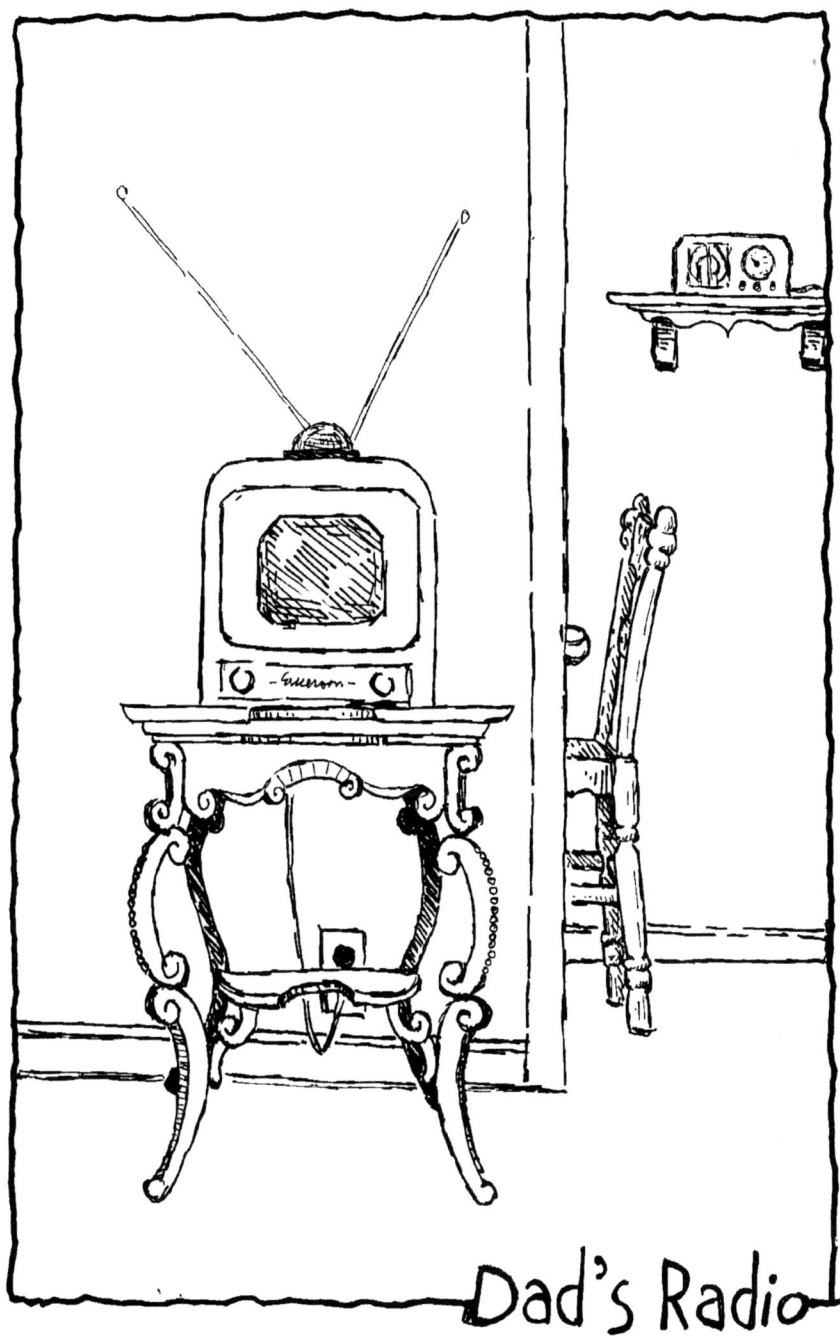

Dad's Radio

Dad's Radio

Dad loved listening to "The Shadow" and "The Green Hornet" on his radio. We had to be very quiet so we didn't disturb his concentration.

"The Shadow" was scary. There were squeaky doors, sounds of feet running, gun shots, screams, wind storms and crashes. I was allowed to stay up and listen because Dad said it would feed my imagination

The radio was a rectangular box made out of fancy carved wood. It had a screen over the front where sound came out, and dials to turn for changing stations.

The radio sat on an antique table across from the couch, just like TVs do now.

Mom didn't like the radio. She preferred playing 78 records on the Victrola. The records were circular and about 10 inches across. They had a hole in the middle and were black. Grooves were cut into the record. When a needle was placed in a groove and the turntable started, music played. It was scratchy sounding, but you could hear violins, piano, trumpets and singing.

Those records came before CDs, before cassettes, before 45 records and before 33 1/3 albums. You see them now in old movies or living museums.

Dad listened to radio and mom played her records. Then someone in our neighborhood got a television set. Soon, several families had them. The families who didn't have a new "TV" were jealous.

On Saturday nights, dad's friend, who lived behind us and always borrowed dad's tools, invited us over to see "Milton Berle's Texaco Star Theater." We went for five Saturdays. Then dad wouldn't go anymore. He said he felt like a leech, which I found out later was a terrible, blood-sucking creature.

That night, mom and dad talked for a long, long time in their room, whispery-like. For a week they whispered.

Then, early Saturday morning, Dad went downtown. He hated going downtown on weekends because he worked there every day. When he came home he had a "TV." It had a rounded front about the size of today's computer monitors. The back stuck out my arm's length. You could see a bunch of tubes and wires if you peeked through.

Dad took his radio off the antique table and put it on a shelf in the kitchen. He placed the new television on the fancy antique table, connected a wire from the rabbit ears antennae to the back of the TV, plugged it into the wall, and stood back admiring his purchase.

After a torturous minute of looking, he switched it on. A long time passed before anything happened. Then we could hear words but couldn't see anything. Finally, a picture began to flicker on the screen. At first it was dim, then it got brighter and brighter. We stared. Amazing! People moved and talked, all in black and white like a newspaper.

Dad invited the neighbors over to watch Milton Berle at our house. A lot of times after that, I got to turn the channel button on the front of the TV because Dad didn't want to get out of his chair.

Dad still listened to "The Shadow Knows" and Mom still listened to music, but the radio never regained its dominant position in the house.

The Rockettes

The Rockettes

A spectacular day! I got to wear my braids up on top of my head with a bow and my patent leather party shoes. I wore a white dress with red stripes because red went with Christmas, and we were going to the "Radio City Christmas Spectacular."

The train into the city whizzed and lurched. As we got closer to Manhattan, more people boarded—tall and short folks, Chinese, black, Indian and Japanese. One oriental mom, wearing a fancy gold dress with a collar that stuck up, was taking her son to Radio City, too. As the crowd was pouring out of the subway train and climbing the stairs toward the light, Mom spoke excitedly. "You'll love it," she said, with that tone of assurance that one never questioned. Her eyes lit up, and she pushed me along the street. "There'll be a movie," she continued breathlessly, "then singers, dancers and music. You'll love it."

We turned the corner toward Radio City. Glitter assaulted us. A Christmas tree four stories tall flickered with millions of white lights. The marquee on the building read, "Radio City Music Hall, featuring the Rockettes." Red velvet ropes kept the huge line of people orderly as they waited. When the doors opened, a crush of children in Sunday clothes, mothers with smiles, and Dads looking tolerant entered the elaborate lobby.

From our balcony seats, first row center, I gazed at the huge stage, a gigantic organ, and at least 50 Christmas trees lining the stage and ramps. I don't remember the movie. After it was over, I could hear everyone holding their breath waiting for the giant red velvet curtain to open. It didn't. A cymbal crashed, and down the aisle pranced at least 40 beautiful women, all dressed alike in red outfits with short skirts and white fur hats, like miniature Santa Clauses. Their identical silver shoes clicked as they ascended onto the stage. They danced, tapping together, kicking their legs together, turning their heads together, twirling together and ending up in the splits together. I gasped.

Mom was right. I loved it. The velvet curtain opened, revealing a Christmas tree with people on it instead of ornaments, and gift packages as big as dining room tables. A handsome boy in a tuxedo sang "Santa Claus Is Coming to Town," and actresses in long skirts—like they wore 100 years ago—danced with young men in tights. The Rockettes tapped their way around them; then the lights dimmed.

But it wasn't over. After a singer and a guy dressed up like a bear, they were back. They wore white, bell-shaped dresses made of net. You could see their legs move under the white hoops, all together at the same time. The singer sang. The music got louder and louder. The tapping got faster and faster, until, bang! A huge gong sounded. The lights went out. Poof, the costumes lit up with blinking white lights, and the stage was a sea of female Christmas Trees tapping to the music. It was the most beautiful thing I'd ever seen! The music, the costumes, the dancing, the joy. This is what life is supposed to be, I thought.

The audience stood and cheered. The ladies bowed and left the stage. After a comedian, they came back three times—once as toy soldiers, once as characters from the Christmas Story, and, at the end, back in their red and white costumes. I was transported. I wanted to **be** them. I wanted to stay in that world. It was hard going home. The music, the lights, the costumes—it was magic. And from that moment on I knew I had to be part of that magic world. Somehow I would find a way.

The June Bug

The June Bug

I admired bugs. Red and black ladybugs visited the flowers regularly. They took sunbaths while perched on a fluttering leaf. They could crawl and fly. And when you got one in your hand, it didn't seem frightened.

Spiders had lots of legs and could fly through the air without wings. Watching them weave a web could eliminate a whole hour of boredom. Even the sand roaches, which sent my mother screaming for the Raid, were interesting. They had short bodies that looked like stubby cigars with long antennae.

I had never met a disgusting bug until *the June bug*. We had moved again, further into the country. When my brother discovered his friends could terrify their mothers, their sisters, their grandmothers and their girlfriends by simply shaking an evil looking bug in their face, he rushed home, eager to test it on me. Imagine his disappointment when he captured a spider, thrust it at me, and I said, "Interesting hairy legs." Not exactly what he'd planned. He tried caterpillars, worms, garden snakes and beetles. Nothing worked.

As summer approached, a whole new variety of creatures populated our yard. There were more mosquitoes than I had ever seen, so screen doors were a must. On hot afternoons, a whole collection of beetle-like creatures collected on the screen door. "They're June Bugs," said a neighbor. "They like the cool air coming from inside, and they'll hang on the screen until the temperature drops.

One hot, muggy afternoon, my brother said, "I have something for you." He grinned devilishly and dropped a June Bug down my back. The poor thing must have been scared to death. It squeezed its pinchers into my skin—as if my back were the screen door—and it held on for dear life. I screamed. Lew smiled, triumphant. I tried to reach it over my shoulder. It was too far down. I tried to reach it up my back. It was too far up. It clung to just that place I couldn't reach—and it clung and clung and clung. I screamed for Lew to get it off. He laughed. I threatened to kill him. He laughed more. I begged. He laughed. I cried. He laughed. All I could think of was getting rid of that bug. I rubbed up against the wall. Nothing. I tried a rolling pin. Nothing. He laughed. I grabbed the broom and went after him. He ran outside, me right behind him, broom extended.

Screaming, sobbing and sniveling, I arrived at the neighbor's, where Mom was having a nice, quiet tea. She had trouble understanding what I was talking about. The neighbor laughed quietly, lifted up my shirt and plucked the June Bug off my back. "It's a favorite boy's trick around here," she explained to my mother. "It only works once."

But she was wrong. I never got over it.

The Violin

The Violin Lessons

Every Monday, as soon as school let out, I'd run to the car. Mom and I headed for Manhattan. We went to a famous school where I took violin lessons. I called it "Julia's" but most adults knew it as Julliard. It was a flood of music. Music floated everywhere. Piano music. Violin music. Horn music. Oboe music. Percussion music. College students practiced in little rooms that looked like cells, in hallways, in the restroom, and even in their cars. Except for two other kids, the students were all adults.

My teacher was a large man with eyes as dark as my bedroom with the lights out. He had wild, black, curly hair that jumped around like springs when he shook his head. At first he frightened me. He reminded me of a troll. Then he grinned and giggled. I giggled. My mother giggled. Then we were friends.

Each week when I arrived, I'd run over, give him a hug, and he'd giggle. He'd grill me about practicing, and his eyes would look like black coals sizzling in Dad's bar-b-que. Then he'd shake his head, sending black curls in every direction— like 100 slinky toys. He made me work hard. At the end of every lesson, he'd play for me.

When he played the violin, he'd close his eyes and sway. His curly hair flopped around like a dog shaking off water. He could make the melody of a nursery rhyme sound like angels playing tag. Every note was crisp and clear and danced off the strings.

I tried hard to learn. After a while, my sounds weren't horrid squeaks anymore. They began to sound like music. I began to sway. He'd smile and giggle. The better I liked a piece, the more I'd sway, and the more he'd giggle. Then I'd sneeze. He'd say, "God Bless, for it is God who gives the gift." I sneezed a lot, so he said that a lot. Sometimes I'd sneeze and wheeze all the way home from the lesson.

Eventually, I was ready. He took me into an auditorium bigger than our school library. The only other kid, a boy about 10, played a horn with lots of curls in the middle. My teacher said if I played well, he'd give me tickets to Radio City.

I listened to three women singers, two piano players and a short lady playing half a flute. Then, it was my turn. All I could think about was those tickets. I tried not to sway or sneeze, and I played wonderfully until a string broke on my violin. He always told me, "No matter what, just keep playing." So I did. But I knew those tickets were gone. When I finished, I didn't even wait for clapping. I ran and sat down.

But people clapped a lot, and the master of the school came over and said something about transposing and stage presence, and I could see my teacher smiling. Then I sneezed. I sneezed five times, until my mother had to take me out.

The next week I went to the doctor twice because of my asthma, and I missed three days of school. I missed my music lesson, too. When I went back to "Julia's," he gave me a really hard piece. I practiced it a lot at home. Then we had to cancel the lesson because I was sick again.

Mom said my violin playing aggravated my asthma. That night, I took my violin to bed.

The next time I went to a lesson, my teacher gave me those tickets and some new stuff to rub on my bow so I wouldn't sneeze. The new stuff didn't help. Whenever I played the violin, the asthma came. Each time I'd sneeze or wheeze, he'd say, "God bless, for it is God who gives the gift."

The doctor said I had to quit. My teacher cried when he said good-bye. His curly black hair hung down, and he didn't giggle. I never saw him again. And I never did understand why if God gave the gift he would also give me asthma. It took away my violin and fun things like softball, running track and raking leaves. It even took away my dad's job because we had to move.

Moving again

Moving Again

Dad figured everything out almost to the minute. Dad would follow the moving van in our Kaiser. That would take three to four days. He'd find an apartment, report for his new job, and get settled. We'd spend two weeks at Silver Beach with Grandma, then fly out west. We'd get there August 20th, just in time to register for school.

It was exciting. We weren't just moving to another house this time. We were moving thousands of miles away to a place where everybody wore cowboy hats and boots. We'd looked at the pictures and the maps a hundred times. Dad's two favorite places were Texas and Arizona. Texas had cows with gigantic heads, called Longhorns. Arizona had prickly things called Saguaro Cactus. Dad got a job offer in Texas first, so that's where we were headed.

Mom said she was going to get a job, too, since Lew and I were more grown up. She had an offer already to work as assistant manager at a big bookstore in Dallas. But she was sad, too. She had to leave her piano at Grandma's house.

We threw away lots of stuff—old toys, clothes we'd outgrown, old books from Mom's college years, even some furniture. A big van marked "NY Salvation Army" came and got most of it. Lew tried to take back his train set, but dad gave him a "look" and the pout went away. Mom gave away all her kitchen dishes and only took her best china, wrapped in a dozen layers of newspaper. That meant we had to eat off paper plates until we got some other "everyday" dishes.

The moving truck came. I still wasn't dressed when it arrived, so I had to rush and put on clothes so the moving men wouldn't see me in my pajamas. We only got to keep one suitcase for each of us. I threw my PJs into a box that the moving men whisked away. They whisked away everything into that big hole, bigger than all the other moving trucks we'd ever seen.

Dad had the car packed so tight you could barely see out the rear view mirror. He had all his clothes, his engineering tools, family papers and a set of golf clubs. It reminded me of the circus when 25 clowns got out of a teeny, tiny car. Before he and the moving van left, dad picked around in the car and retrieved a big bag. Out of it he pulled a cowboy hat and a western shirt for Lew and me. "You have to get used to looking like and thinking like a westerner," he said. He and the big moving van pulled out. There was a little part of me that felt uncomfortable as I looked after them and then at the house with the "For Sale" sign in front.

A taxi pulled up and crammed our three suitcases in the trunk while mom locked the door for the last time. We piled in and headed for Silver Beach. Grandma was glad to see us and had chocolate milk and oatmeal cookies ready. We stayed there almost two weeks. I'd miss Silver Beach, but it had never been the same since Buster left, so I didn't cry. Mom cried. Grandma cried. Lew just wanted to get going. He had on his cowboy hat, a western shirt and a set of toy guns grandma had bought him the day before. He was ready for his new life.

"We're gonna fly to Texas," Lew kept telling every neighbor who came to say goodbye. He kept saying that all the way to the airport. But when he saw the big plane with the huge propellers and heard all the noise, he suddenly got quiet. That's when I got excited. Flying like a bird high over the ground? That sounded like heaven to me.

The pilot invited us into the cockpit. He gave Lew some wings to wear on his western shirt. I thought I was too old for that and said, "No thank you." The stewardess showed us our seats. Lew looked a little green, wings and all. Mom was grinning. She loved new adventures and getting away from the Eastern Establishment had been a dream of hers. I took the window seat and stared as the motors revved up and the propellers twirled faster and faster. Lew hid his face in mom's lap. Mom and I held hands and smiled big smiles as the plane lumbered down the runway and slowly lifted into the sky, carrying us west to our new life.

CONCLUSION

The Albright family moved West in 1949. The author, Penny, did overcome her asthma and get better. She graduated from high school in Scottsdale, Arizona, and got BA and MA degrees from Arizona State University.

Her experience with The Rockettes influenced her decision to teach theatre, English and public speaking for 30 years. During that time she directed, acted in, and worked tech on hundreds of theatre productions. She has also written several plays that have been produced.

After three decades in educational theatre, Penny retired to become an author and playwright. Her first book, *Letters to My Aunt*, is in its second printing, and she has had several of her plays produced in local community theater settings.

This collection of remembrances was originally created for her grandchildren.

Wanna write down some of the stuff you remember (or will want to remember) from when you were little? Here's a place to do it. Just copy this page as many times as you want

_____

_____

_____

_____

_____

_____

_____

_____

_____

_____

_____

_____

_____

_____

Have you seen Penny Petersen's *other book?*

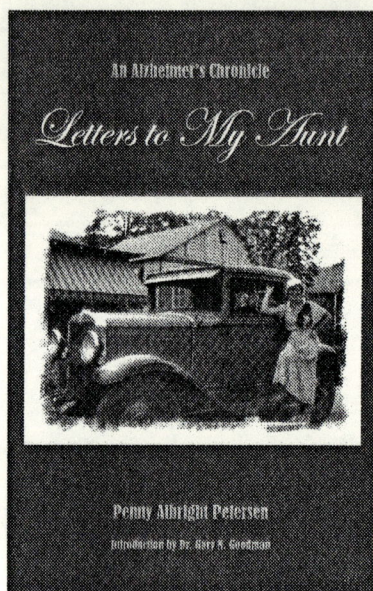

Letters to My Aunt is the chronicle of a loving daughter's sacrifices and triumphs of spirit while caring for her aging mother, an Alzheimer's patient. Ordering information appears on the following page.

Additional copies of this book and/or *Letters to My Aunt*, also by Penny Petersen, may be ordered through your local bookstore, or you may order directly from Desert State Publishing, 9834 Watford Way, Sun Lakes, Arizona 85248.

Please send your check or money order for $17.50 per book, which will cover all costs including shipping and handling.

To order online, go to the OPA Publishing website, http://www.opapresents.com, where you may order using a credit card.